GRIZZLY BEAR

illustrated by Lynne Cherry

E. P. DUTTON • NEW YORK

3 50

PROPERTY OF
BACA GRANDE LIBRARY

D1024679

Wake up, sleepy grizzly bears.
It is spring,
time to come out of your den.

The bears are hungry.
Berries and bark,
meat and fish,
grizzlies eat most anything.

The cubs climb.
The cubs dig.

Fat and furry,
roly-poly,
they grow and grow.
Mother bear looks after her cubs.

So the summer passes.
The grizzly bears choose a new den.
It is time to sleep.

for Doug Mink,
my good friend and fellow explorer of rivers

Text copyright © 1987 by E. P. Dutton
Illustrations copyright © 1987 by Lynne Cherry

All rights reserved.
Licensed by World Wildlife Fund®

Published in the United States by E. P. Dutton,
2 Park Avenue, New York, N.Y. 10016

Published simultaneously in Canada by
Fitzhenry & Whiteside Limited, Toronto

Text and editing: Lucia Monfried   Designer: Isabel Warren-Lynch

Printed in Singapore by Tien Wah Press
First Edition   CUSA & P   10 9 8 7 6 5 4 3 2 1

Library of Congress Cataloging-in-Publication Data

Cherry, Lynne.
  Grizzly bear.

  (Help save us books)
  Summary: A grizzly bear wakes up to spring, looks
after her cubs, and as winter approaches digs a new den.
  1. Grizzly bear—Pictorial works—Juvenile literature.
[1. Grizzly bear.   2. Bears]   I. Monfried, Lucia.
II. Title.   III. Series.
QL737.C27C47   1987   599.74'446   86-24035
ISBN 0-525-44295-2